# HAUNTED CAR

ROGER HURN

BY ROGER HURN

ILLUSTRATED BY MARK PENMAN

# FULL FLIGHT

**Titles in the Full Flight Thrills and Spills series:**

| | |
|---|---|
| The Knight Olympics | Jonny Zucker |
| Pied Piper of London | Danny Pearson |
| The Science Project | Jane A C West |
| Gorilla Thriller | Richard Taylor |
| Clone Zone | Jillian Powell |
| Clowning Around | Helen Orme |
| Time to go Home | David Orme |
| Haunted Car | Roger Hurn |
| Dinosaur Rampage | Craig Allen |
| Rubbish Ghost | Jillian Powell |

Badger Publishing Limited
Oldmedow Road, Hardwick
Industrial Estate, King's
Lynn PE30 4JJ Telephone:
01438 791037
www.badgerlearning.co.uk

4 6 8 10 9 7 5

Haunted Car ISBN 978 1 84926 987 2

Text © Roger Hurn 2013
Complete work © Badger Publishing Limited 2013
Second edition © 2014

The right of Roger Hurn to be identifi ed as author of this
Work has been asserted by him in accordance with the
Copyright, Designs and Patents Act 1988.

Publisher: Susan Ross
Senior Editor: Danny Pearson
Designer: Fiona Grant
Illustrator: Mark Penman

# HAUNTED CAR

BY ROGER HURN

## Contents

Badger
L E A R N I N G

## New words:

| | |
|---|---|
| hitch | thunderstorm |
| paralysed | passenger |
| jackhammer | terrified |
| supernatural | shattered |

## Main characters:

Steve

The Haunted Car

# CHAPTER 1

# A Stormy Night

Steve was totally fed up.

His mates had left him behind at a party and he had no way of getting home. Now he was standing on the side of a lonely road trying to hitch a ride.

It was a really dark night and no cars had passed him for ages.

Suddenly, the inky blackness was lit up by a jagged flash of lightning.

"Oh no, a thunderstorm," he said to himself. "That's the last thing I need."

Thunder rolled across the sky and rain lashed down.

Steve groaned. He didn't have an umbrella. In a matter of seconds, his thin jacket, jeans and shoes were soaking wet.

"I may as well just start walking," he muttered. It was raining so hard he could barely see his hand in front of his face.

He shook his head sadly. Even if a car did come along, the driver wouldn't be able to see him. And even if they did, no driver was going to stop and give him a ride. He was far too wet. Steve sighed.

As he started walking, a car appeared from out of the darkness. It was moving very slowly and its engine was silent.

The pouring rain splashed into Steve's eyes. This made it hard for him to see the car very clearly. But Steve didn't care.

"Hey, some kind person is stopping to give me a lift," he said excitedly. "Maybe this is my lucky night after all!"

He pulled the passenger door open and leapt inside the car.

"Thanks for stopping," he shouted above the din of the wind and rain. "Sorry I'm so wet. I'll try not to drip water all over the seat."

He slammed the door shut against the furious weather. Then he turned to smile at the driver. "Hey, it's good of..."

The words died in his mouth. There was nobody behind the wheel! Steve was alone in the car!

# CHAPTER 2

# The Drop

Steve's mouth fell open. He was rigid with fear.

He no longer cared if he dripped water onto the seat.

"It's a ghost car," he thought. "That's why I didn't hear it. But what does it want with me? And where is it taking me?"

Steve had no answers to these questions, but he was certain the car was evil and that it meant to do him harm.

The car continued to move forward slowly.

Steve was far too terrified to even think of jumping out and running away.

Then, as he stared out through the rain-splattered windscreen, he saw that the car was approaching a sharp bend in the road!

The sight filled Steve with dread.

The road ran alongside a steep drop.

At the side of the road was a fence made of thin wire.

"That fence is hopeless," he gasped. "It will never stop the car from falling over the edge!"

Things were looking grim. Steve was sure the ghost car was going to go off the road, crash through the wire and plummet down the side of the mountain.

Steve had seen this happen in movies and the car always burst into flames.

Now Steve really began to panic. "Oh no," he cried. "Please don't do this. I'm too young to die!"

# CHAPTER 3

# A Pale Hand

At that very moment, a pale hand appeared through the driver's window.

Steve felt fear running up and down his spine like icy fingers. He gulped, then held his breath.

He was sure the hand was coming straight for him.

But it wasn't. Instead, the hand grabbed the steering wheel.

It turned the wheel and guided the car safely around the bend.

Then, as soon as the car was back on track, the hand disappeared back out of the window.

Steve's heart was pounding like a jackhammer but he couldn't move his arms or his legs.

He was paralysed with fright.

The haunted car continued its silent journey.

Every time it reached a bend in the road, Steve was sure it would crash. But the pale hand always came in through the window and turned the steering wheel just in time.

"Why are you doing this to me?" whimpered Steve. "Are you trying to scare me to death? Because, if you are, it's working. I can't take much more of this!"

Steve knew time was running out.

It seemed to him that the ghost car was playing with him like a cat plays with a mouse.

He knew that whatever evil thing was haunting the car would soon get bored and then the pale hand would steer the car over the edge.

"I have got to do something," he muttered. "I am not going to let a ghost car get the better of me."

He forced himself to take deep breaths to calm his shattered nerves.

Slowly, he flexed his fingers and then moved his legs. They felt as wobbly as jelly but at least they moved when he wanted them to.

"OK, Steve," he murmured to himself. "You've got one chance at this, so don't mess it up."

He summoned up his courage but kept his mind blank. He didn't want the car to know what it was he was about to do.

Then he pulled on the door handle and jumped out of the car. Luckily, it wasn't going very fast.

Steve rolled over and leapt back up on to his feet. As he did so, he heard a cry of rage mixed in with the howling wind.

"It's the car," he said to himself. "It knows I've beaten it and it's furious!"

Luckily, he had not hurt himself when he fell. He raced off down the road as fast as he could, without so much as a backward glance.

# Chapter 4

# The Café

Steve didn't stop running until he came to a roadside café.

The bright yellow from the windows
and the pink light from its neon
sign blazed like a beacon into the
dark night.

He looked through the windows at the
people sitting there laughing and
chatting.

He breathed a huge sigh of relief.
This was no ghost café.

He charged inside. "I need a hot, strong cup of tea with plenty of sugar," he yelled. "And I need it now!"

All the other customers stopped talking and stared at this crazy, young guy. Steve stood there, still shaking with fear.

"Hey," said the waitress, "you look like you've seen a ghost!"

Steve nodded. "I have," he said.

Then, in a voice raw with horror, he told the whole café about his supernatural experience.

Every one of the people there felt the hairs stand up on the back of their necks.

When he finished his tale, a terrible silence filled the room.

All the people in the café looked at each other and swallowed hard.

They felt sure that Steve wasn't crazy. His story sounded so real – he must be telling them the truth!

# Chapter 5

## The Strangers

Suddenly, the door to the café opened and two men walked in. They stopped and shook the rain from their coats.

One of the men looked around the café. He wondered why it was so quiet. Then he saw Steve standing at the counter.

He did a double-take and nudged his friend hard in the ribs. He pointed angrily at Steve.

"Hey," he said, "there's that guy who jumped in our broken-down car when we were pushing it in the rain!"

"That's right!" said the other man. "You've got a real cheek, pal. You didn't even offer to lend us a hand! You just grabbed a free ride out of the rain!"

## How to Write a Scary Story

Use these tips to help you write a scary story.

• Think about what scares you. If you're scared of the bogeyman jumping out of the cupboard or a giant spider lurking in your house – then use that as the starting point for your scary story.

• Decide who the main character is going to be. Will it be you or a fictional person? Whoever it is, it must be someone you can understand and identify with.

• Grab the reader's attention by thinking up a great setting. A scary story needs lots of spooky atmosphere and tension.

• Your setting doesn't have to be an old house or a spooky castle. It could be in a supermarket or even your school. When something unusual happens in an ordinary place it can be really creepy!

- Think up some 'What if?' questions: What if you were alone in a dark wood? What if you heard strange noises…?

- Develop and describe your main characters. What are their strengths and weaknesses? Why are they acting as they do?

- Show what is happening, don't just tell it. For example,

  **Tell**

  *The spider came down the corridor.*

  **Show**

  *The huge and very hairy spider scuttled down the corridor snapping its fearsome jaws!*

- Give your scary story an ending that is satisfying. It must resolve the suspense – either in a good or a bad way.

## Questions about the Story

What was Steve trying to do?

What was the weather like?

Why didn't Steve hear the car?

Why was Steve scared when he sat in the passenger seat?

What did Steve think was going to happen to the car?

Why didn't the car crash when it came to a bend in the road?

What did Steve hear when he jumped out of the car?

Where did Steve go after he ran away from the car?

Steve thought the car was haunted. What was the real story?